Published by Ladybird Books Ltd Loughborough Leicestershire UK
Ladybird Books Inc Auburn Maine 04210 USA

© LADYBIRD BOOKS LTD MCMLXXXIV

Printed in England

Humpty Dumpty

and other nursery rhymes

Illustrated by KEN McKIE

Ladybird Books

Humpty Dumpty sat on a wall,
Humpty Dumpty had a great fall,
All the king's horses,
And all the king's men,
Couldn't put Humpty together again.

Little Jack Horner
Sat in a corner,
Eating his Christmas pie;
He put in his thumb,
And pulled out a plum,
And said, "What a good boy am I!"

Baa, baa, black sheep,
Have you any wool?
Yes, sir, yes, sir,
Three bags full;
One for the master,
And one for the dame,
And one for the little boy
Who lives down the lane.

*P*at-a-cake, pat-a-cake,
     baker's man,

Bake me a cake,
     as fast as you can;

Pat it and prick it
     and mark it with B,

And put it in the oven
     for baby and me.

Jack be nimble,
Jack be quick,
Jack jump over
The candlestick.

To market, to market,
to buy a fat pig,

Home again, home again,
jiggety-jig;

To market, to market,
to buy a fat hog,

Home again, home again,
jiggety-jog.

*S*ee-saw, Margery Daw,

Johnny shall have
a new master;

He shall have
but a penny a day,

Because he can't work
any faster.

*T*here was an old woman
who lived in a shoe,

She had so many children
she didn't know what to do;

She gave them some broth
without any bread;

Then whipped them all soundly
and sent them to bed.

What are little boys made of?
Frogs and snails
And puppy-dogs' tails,
That's what little boys are made of.

What are little girls made of?
Sugar and spice
And all that's nice,
That's what little girls are made of.

Three blind mice, see how they run!

They all ran after the farmer's wife;

She cut off their tails
with a carving knife,

Did ever you see such
a thing in your life,

As three blind mice?

Lucy Locket lost her pocket,
Kitty Fisher found it;
Not a penny was there in it,
But a ribbon round it.

Two little dicky birds
Sat upon a wall;
One named Peter
The other named Paul.
Fly away, Peter!
Fly away, Paul!
Come back, Peter!
Come back, Paul!

There was a little girl,
*   and she had a little curl,*

Right in the middle
*   of her forehead;*

When she was good,
*   she was very, very good,*

But when she was bad,
*   she was horrid.*

The north wind doth blow,
And we shall have snow,
And what will poor robin do then?
    Poor thing!

He'll sit in a barn,
And keep himself warm,
And hide his head under his wing.
    Poor thing!

Goosey, goosey gander,
Where shall I wander?
Upstairs and downstairs
And in my lady's chamber.
There I met an old man
Who would not say his prayers,
I took him by the left leg
And threw him down the stairs.

Mary had a little lamb,
Its fleece was white as snow;
And everywhere that Mary went
The lamb was sure to go.

It followed her to school one day,
That was against the rule;
It made the children laugh and play
To see a lamb at school.

Tom, he was a piper's son,

He learned to play
when he was young,

But all the tune
that he could play

Was, "Over the hills
and far away."

Over the hills and
a great way off,

The wind will blow
my top-knot off.

Tom with his pipe
made such a noise,

That he pleased both
the girls and boys,

And they all stopped
to hear him play,

"Over the hills and far away."

There was a crooked man,
     and he walked a crooked mile,

He found a crooked sixpence
     against a crooked stile;

He bought a crooked cat,
     which caught a crooked mouse,

And they all lived together
     in a little crooked house.

Simple Simon met a pieman,
Going to the fair,
Says Simple Simon to the pieman,
Let me taste your ware.

Says the pieman to Simple Simon,
Show me first your penny;
Says Simple Simon to the pieman,
Indeed I have not any.

Simple Simon went a-fishing,
For to catch a whale;
All the water he had got
Was in his mother's pail.

Simple Simon went to look
If plums grew on a thistle,
He pricked his finger very much;
Which made poor Simon whistle.

I had a little pony,
His name was Dapple Grey:
I lent him to a lady
To ride a mile away.

She whipped him, she lashed him,
She rode him through the mire;
I would not lend my pony now,
For all the lady's hire.